MW00933566

THE Little Lion That Listened

Written by Nicholas Tana
Illustrated by Jessie Fox
Story Design by Matthew Molleur

Library of Congress Cataloguing-in-Publication Data
Tana, Nicholas.
The Little Lion That Listened/Nicholas Tana; illustrated by Jessie Fox.

Summary: Little Leo is a great listener.
His listening skills even save his family from danger.
But Leo refuses to roar. His father worries that Leo will never earn the respect of the other animals.
Only Leo's mother believes her son will roar when he is ready. Will Leo find his voice when his family needs him most?

Library of Congress Control Number:
2021913455

ISBN 978-1-950033-15-7

First edition

The illustrations in this book were done in Procreate.
The text was set in Roboto Slab.
Layout design by Matthew Molleur.

Dedicated to my lovely
muse and daughter, Cat. You help me to listen.
From Nicholas Tana

Dedicated to Clyde and Nancy, from Jessie
And to Joseph and Suzanne, from Matt

Little Leo
didn't roar like his
brother and sister.

His brother could
roar loudly.

His sister could roar
for a long time.

But Leo
didn't seem
to roar
at all.

This made Leo's father nervous.

"Nobody will ever respect a quiet lion," he complained.

Even Leo's brother and sister thought it was strange.

"He will
grow up to roar
when he is ready,"
said his mother.

One day, Leo's mother took the three cubs into the jungle to learn to hunt.

While Leo's family stalked a gazelle, Leo heard a rustling in the nearby bushes.

Leo heard hunters approaching.
Quietly, he pointed them out to his mother.
Thanks to Leo, they all escaped unharmed.

When Leo and his family arrived home,
Leo's father was happy to know they were safe.

"It's a good thing Leo was listening," said his mother.

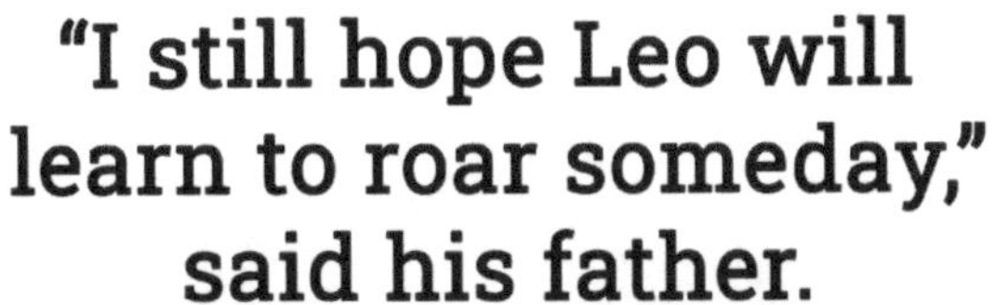

"I still hope Leo will learn to roar someday," said his father.

"Leo will learn to roar when he is ready," encouraged his mother.

One night, Leo woke
to hear his brother and sister
playing in the jungle.

They were so busy playing
they didn't hear the approaching hyenas.

Leo heard them and pointed out their shadowy figures.
Thanks to Leo, they were able to sneak away unnoticed.

"If it wasn't for Leo,
we might have been eaten!"
said Leo's brother.

His sister agreed
and gave Leo a big hug.

They were so
tired and scared they all
fell asleep under the stars
while Leo listened to
the crickets chirping.

The next morning,
they awoke very thirsty and lost.
They felt too weak to roar for help

In the distance, Leo heard the sound of running water.

He raced toward it and
his brother and sister followed.
They came upon a stream
and drank from it.

Feeling stronger, Leo's brother and sister roared.

Leo's brother roared loudly.

Leo's sister roared for a long time.

They roared so loudly their parents heard them.
"It's a good thing we could hear you both roaring," said their mother.

"I wish Leo would learn to roar, too,"
said their father.

One morning, Leo's father woke up very excited.

It was time for the Yearly Lion Roaring Competition!

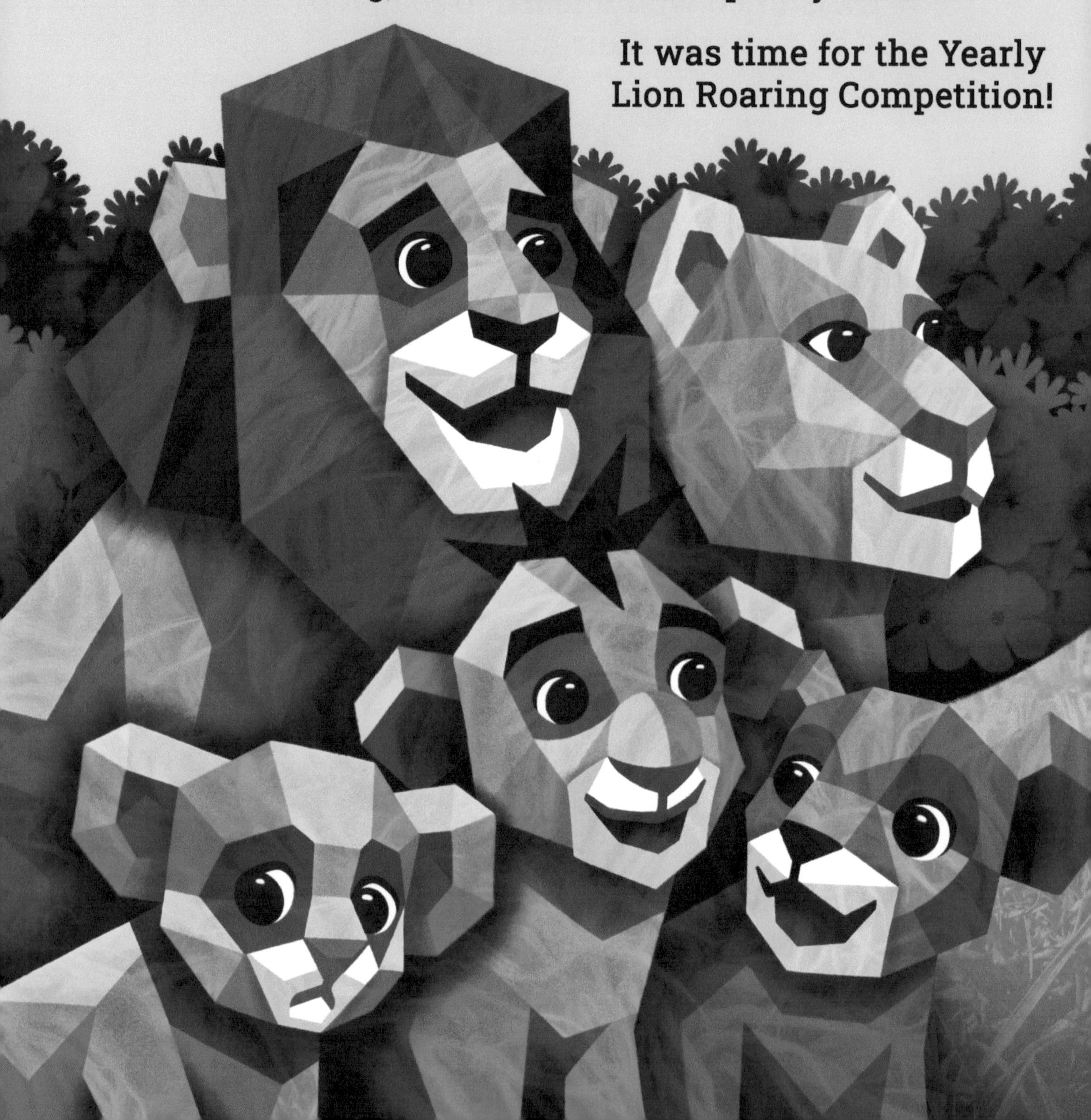

Leo's father
was proud because
he had once won the competition.
He hoped one of his children would win it, too.

During the competition,
Leo's brother roared the loudest.

Leo's sister roared
the longest.

But Leo
never
roared
at all.

"Why can't you roar like your brother and sister?" Leo's father shouted.

Feeling ashamed,
Leo ran away.
He climbed up a hill.

From up high, Leo could still hear the lions roaring.
Then in the distance, he heard crackling...

The jungle was on fire!

Although Leo was safely high in the hills, he worried about his family.

The fire was moving rapidly towards the other lions below.

Leo knew he
had to warn them.

He took a deep breath...
and roared.

Leo roared very loudly
and for so long.

"Look! It's Leo!" shouted his father.

Thanks to Leo,
the other lions noticed
the fire. They scurried
up the hill to join Leo
where it was safe.

“I can’t believe how loud Leo roared!” said his brother.

“I can’t believe how long Leo roared!” said his sister.

“I can’t believe Leo roared at all!” said his father.

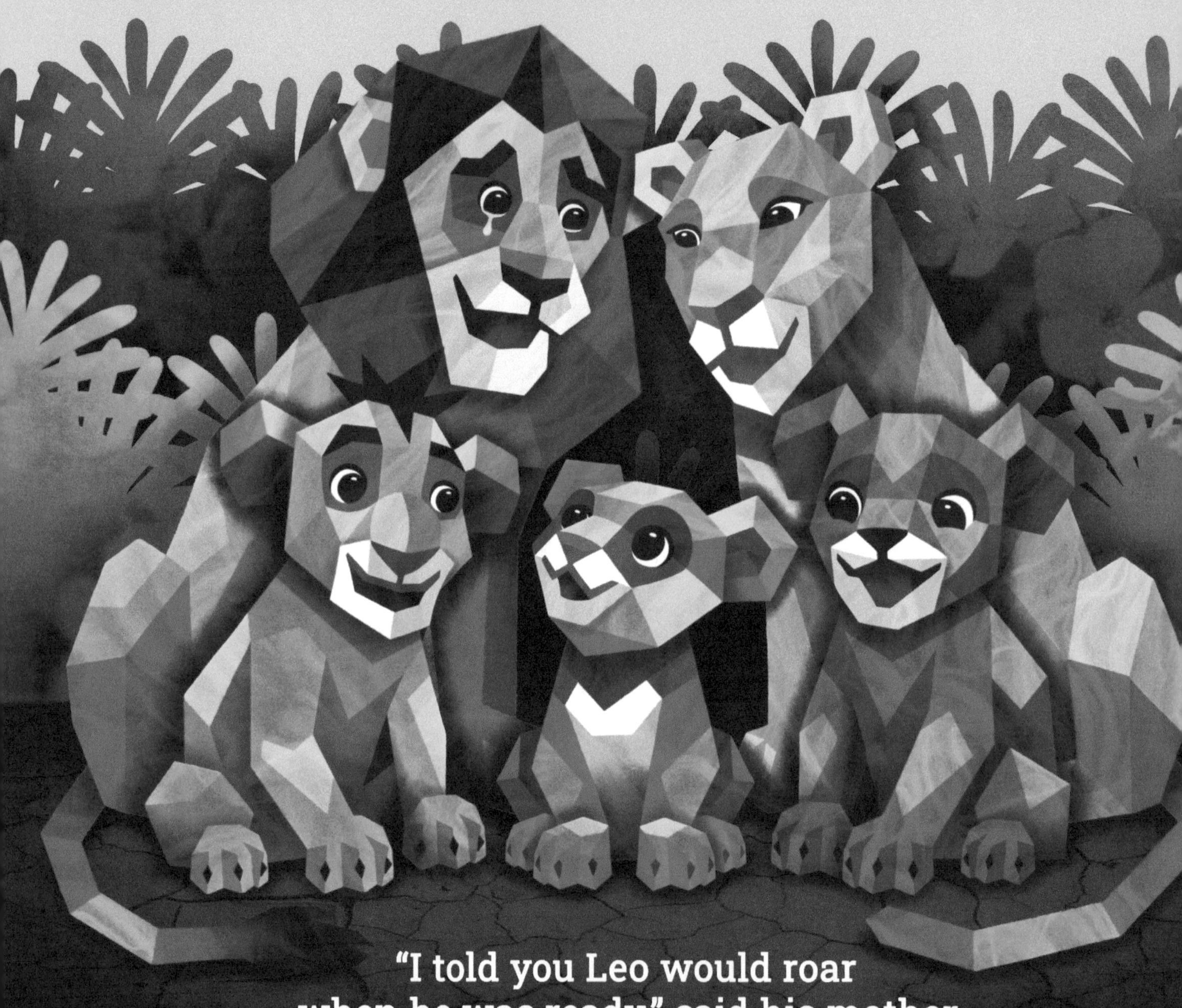

“I told you Leo would roar when he was ready,” said his mother.

After that day, Leo became famous throughout the jungle.
While the other lions thanked him, guess what Leo did.

He listened.

The End

Nicholas Tana is an award-winning writer, director, and musician. He is the author of "Monsters Are Afraid of Babies", "The Kitten, The Cat, and The Apple", and "The Kingdom of Glee". Tana's original Snow White Story, "Snow White and the Wishing Well", appears in Disney's 5 Minute Easter Stories.

Jessie Fox is an Arizona-based illustrator. She has been drawing obsessively since the age of three and is currently pursuing her degree in graphic design. Jessie has a passion for illustration, books, and libraries. This is her first published children's book.

Matthew Molleur is a digital illustrator focused on comic book style art, animation, and motion graphics, and is the 2012 winner of the Pop Culture Paradise 24-hour Comics Day contest. Matt is the illustrator of the children's book "The Kitten, The Cat, and The Apple", as well as the comic book "American Robo" and "Why and How to Make Your Own Comics".

CPSIA information can be obtained
at www.ICGtesting.com
Printed in the USA
BVHW020919270821
615133BV00028B/385

* 9 7 8 1 9 5 0 0 3 3 1 5 7 *